Mickey Mysteries

MYSTERY OF THE SECRET TREASURE

Collect these Mickey Mysteries:

Mystery in Midair

and

Mystery of the Garbage Gang
Available July 2001

Mickey Mysteries

MYSTERY OF THE SECRET TREASURE

DISNEY PRESS

New York

Printed in the United States of America

First edition
1 3 5 7 9 10 8 6 4 2

Library of Congress Catalog Card Number on file
ISBN 0-7868-4450-7

For more Disney Press fun, visit www.disneybooks.com

Chapter 1

PARTY AT HORACE'S HOUSE

"This is going to be so much fun!" Minnie exclaimed from the passenger seat of Mickey's car. "Tonight at Horace's party, we can take a break and forget our detective work for a little while. Robberies, mysterious disappearances, going undercover . . ."

Mickey grinned at his friend as he made his way through the rush-hour traffic. "You're telling me that you're tired of our exciting lifestyle?" Mickey asked in disbelief. "We could always turn our detective agency into a quiet little antiques shop if you want to. . . ."

Minnie burst into laughter.

"Did you hear that, Clarabelle?" Minnie turned around to face their friend in the backseat. "Can you believe what I have to put up with?"

Clarabelle gave a faint half smile.

"What's the matter?" Minnie asked. "We're going to a party! You should be excited."

Clarabelle sighed. "Oh, Minnie, I know," she said. "It's just that I've had some bad news. A few years ago, I took a loan from the bank so I could buy my house. Well, today I got a letter from the bank saying that I have to pay back the outstanding debt in two weeks! I don't think I can do it. I'm worried that the bank is going to take my house away!"

"No!" Minnie looked upset. "They wouldn't do that, would they?"

"They can, and they will," Clarabelle replied. "If I don't pay off my debt, the house will legally belong to the bank. . . ."

Mickey glanced at Clarabelle in the rearview mirror. "Are you sure you don't have enough money to make the payment?" he asked.

"Yes, pretty sure," Clarabelle said, nodding. "About a month ago, I made a terrible investment. What a mistake! I've lost so much money." Clarabelle sighed heavily.

Mickey turned a corner and pulled into Horace's driveway. When he had parked the car and turned off the engine, he turned around in his seat. "Clarabelle," he said firmly, "don't you worry about a thing. Together, you and Minnie and I will figure something out. I promise."

"That's right," Minnie added. "We're here for you if you need any help. Okay?"

"Okay," said Clarabelle. She sniffled, then managed a little smile. "You two are the best."

The three of them got out of the car and walked up the path to the front door. They could already hear the noise from the party inside.

Horace Horsecollar's parties were always a blast, and Clarabelle loved to dance. So the two detectives knew that the moment their friend got inside, she'd forget all about the mortgage on her house—at least for a little while.

And they were right. Within minutes of their arrival, Clarabelle was cutting loose on the dance floor.

"Just as I hoped," Minnie said to Horace as she nibbled on a cheese puff. "Clarabelle seems to be having a wonderful time."

"That's right," said Horace. "Except . . . I sure wish she were dancing with somebody other than Sylvester Slick."

"Me, too," Mickey agreed, joining them.

"Who is Sylvester Slick?" Minnie asked.

"Hmmm. . . ." Horace replied. "I guess I haven't introduced you to him. The second he saw Clarabelle tonight, he walked up and asked her to dance. And from then on . . ." Horace trailed off glumly, shaking his head. Then, realizing he hadn't answered Minnie's question, he added, "I haven't known him long. I met him a few months ago at a party, and he seemed nice enough at the time. Actually, he was the one who suggested I have this party. He wanted to meet my friends. But now . . . I think I made a big mistake!" Horace gazed wistfully at Clarabelle.

"There's just something about him. . . ."

Mickey said. "Minnie, do you remember that case of the fake telephone bills? There was a rumor going around that he was involved."

"Oh, yeah," Minnie said. "How could I have forgotten a name like that? Mr. Slick! I've never seen him in person before. There wasn't any evidence against him, was there, Mickey?"

Mickey shook his head no.

"He sure is a great dancer, though," Minnie continued. "But I suppose it wouldn't be a bad idea to warn Clarabelle about him. Horace, go ask her to dance. Then you can keep an eye on her."

"Humph," Horace replied angrily. "Never!"

"Why not?"

"Well, I already asked her when Sylvester was off getting her a drink," Horace said, blushing slightly. "But she turned me down. She said she had promised to dance with him all night!"

But Minnie wasn't one to give up easily. She spotted Goofy by the refreshment table. He was tapping his foot to the music while biting into a big piece of pie.

The detective walked up to him and explained what she wanted him to do. Goofy was happy to help. He kept a close eye on Clarabelle. Then, when there was a pause in the music and Sylvester excused himself, Goofy marched up to Clarabelle and asked her to dance.

But Sylvester returned almost immediately.

"Clarabelle, allow me to come to your aid!" he said smoothly, wrapping his arm around her waist. "I've seen Goofy's dancing. Believe me, *I'll* be far less likely to step on your feet."

Clarabelle just giggled as Mr. Slick swept her away.

"Unbelievable!" Goofy complained to Minnie a little later as they danced together. "I've never seen Clarabelle like this before!"

"Oh, Goofy," Minnie said, giving her friend's arm a pat, "don't take it personally. She's had a lot on her mind lately."

"Well, she doesn't *look* worried!"

Goofy was right. Clarabelle was positively beaming as she danced with Mr. Slick.

Minnie sighed. "You're right. It seems like

he's really won her over. And they've only
known each other a few hours. Clarabelle is
my friend, but . . . she doesn't seem like herself tonight. Ouch!" Minnie kept dancing, but
she limped a little.

"Sorry, I've never been much of a dancer,"
Goofy said bashfully. "So what is it that's trou-
bling Clarabelle? Can we do anything?"

"It's her house. She has to repay her mortgage, and if she can't do it in time, she might lose her home," answered the investigator. Then she lowered her voice. "I'll explain it all to you later. Right now, they're too close. They might overhear."

The rest of the evening went much the same: Horace sulked in a corner, looking at Clarabelle. Minnie told Goofy the whole story. And Clarabelle and Sylvester danced all night, unable to take their eyes off of each other.

Mickey, meanwhile, watched the entire scene, utterly perplexed.

Chapter 2

STRANGE BEHAVIOR

Horace Horsecollar woke the next morning feeling very sad. The party had been a total disaster—at least for him. He hadn't danced with Clarabelle once. He hadn't even talked to her, really. And when he saw Clarabelle leaving with Sylvester Slick, Horace was so disappointed that he hid in the kitchen so he wouldn't have to say good-bye.

But now he felt awful for being rude. Should I go over to her house to apologize? Horace wondered. No, maybe it would be better to write a note. A short but affectionate letter should fix everything, he decided.

Ten days later, Horace still hadn't heard from Clarabelle. Not a note, not a phone call. Nothing. Finally, Horace summoned his courage and went over to see how she was doing. But by the time he arrived at her house, he wondered if he had made a mistake. What if she slammed the door in his face?

"Be brave, Horace," he said to himself. "Come on—ring the doorbell!" Clarabelle opened the door before he could make up his mind.

"Oh, it's you." She didn't sound particularly happy to see him. "I thought I heard something out here. Hey, what are these flowers doing here?"

Only then did Horace notice the beautiful bunch of red roses sitting just to the side of Clarabelle's front door.

"Red roses!" she scoffed. "How unoriginal."

"But—but . . ." Horace stammered in embarrassment. "I didn't—"

Clarabelle wasn't listening. She had just discovered a note in the flowers, and it was signed Sylvester Slick. "Oh, my goodness!" she

cried happily, running into the house to find a vase.

Horace stepped into the living room. Clarabelle returned from the kitchen and arranged the flowers in the vase carefully. "I should have known these were from Sylvester," she said. "He's always so romantic. Listen to this message:

"Roses for you, my beautiful flower.
Hoping that we will spend the rest of our
lives together."

Clarabelle sighed. "Isn't he wonderful?" she asked dreamily.

Horace didn't reply.

There's no way I'll ever impress Clarabelle now, he thought, completely miserable. Sylvester's really won her over. And judging from the note, it sounded like Sylvester wanted to marry her. What a disaster! If Sylvester was as big a crook as Mickey said he was, someone had to stop Clarabelle from marrying him!

Mr. Slick is after something, Horace realized,

and I'm going to prove it! I'm sure Mickey and Minnie will help me.

Without even pausing to say good-bye, Horace rushed to the Mickey and Minnie Detective Agency and told his friends what he had seen.

"Gosh," Mickey said. "That Mr. Slick is up to no good. It almost seems like he wants to marry Clarabelle to get something out of her. But it couldn't be money—she doesn't have any!"

"Maybe Sylvester doesn't know that," Minnie suggested. She grabbed her coat. "I'm going to see Clarabelle. Maybe I can talk some sense into her about marrying Sylvester. In the meantime, you guys should check out his history."

"Hello, Minnie!" Clarabelle said when she saw her friend at the door. "Come in. Would you like a glass of lemonade?"

"No, thank you, Clarabelle," the detective said as she stepped into the living room. "I came over to discuss something very important with you," Minnie continued. "It's about Sylvester Slick."

"What do you want to tell me about my fiancé?" Clarabelle asked, batting her eyelashes. She giggled when Minnie's mouth dropped open in shock. "That's right, we're thinking about getting married soon!"

"Clarabelle," interrupted the concerned detective, "marriage is a very big deal. You shouldn't just rush into it."

"But it was love at first sight," Clarabelle protested.

"You've only known him for ten days!" Minnie reminded her.

Clarabelle shook her head impatiently. "No, you're wrong."

"What do you mean?" Minnie's forehead wrinkled in confusion.

"I feel like I've known him forever!" Clarabelle explained. "You see, his grandfather, Stephen Slick, was a close friend of my grandfather, Bill Pelton. Have I ever told you about him?"

"Sure," Minnie answered. "'Mineshaft' Bill Pelton, the famous gold prospector."

"That's him! When Sylvester told me that our grandfathers were friends, I knew that our meeting was meant to be. So there's no need for me to watch out for myself. Now, I don't mean to shoo you away, but Sylvester will be here any minute. And you've given me a great idea! We'll look around the attic for Grandpa's old things today. Sylvester mentioned he was interested in doing that. Isn't it marvelous that he's so interested in my family?"

Before the detective had a chance to answer, the doorbell rang.

Clarabelle practically ran to the door. "Hello, darling," she sang out, and a moment later Sylvester followed her into the living room.

They were so busy gazing into one another's eyes that they hardly even seemed to notice that Minnie was still sitting on the couch.

"I guess I ought to go," the detective announced suddenly, grabbing her purse.

"Good-bye, Minnie," Sylvester Slick said, barely even glancing in her direction. "Well, should we head up to the attic?" he asked Clarabelle.

Hearing that, Minnie stopped in her tracks.

"Oh, may I come too, Clarabelle?" she asked. "I love looking through old things."

Sylvester's smile faltered. He checked his watch. "Look at the time! I'm sorry, Clarabelle, but I've got to go. I'm running late for an important meeting."

Clarabelle looked crestfallen as she walked her fiancé to the door.

"Now, why would he rush off like that?" she asked Minnie as soon as Sylvester's car had pulled out of the driveway. "Did I say something wrong? Maybe it's this dress. Oh, I knew I should have worn the blue one...."

Minnie kept quiet. She didn't want to say so, but the detective didn't think that Clarabelle's outfit was the reason Sylvester took off. His "important meeting" was a cover for something else, no doubt about it.

He didn't want me around while he was searching the attic, the investigator thought. I'll bet there's something important up there. Something he wants to keep secret.

"Clarabelle," Minnie said, "let's see what your grandfather has hidden away upstairs."

Chapter 3

THE TREASURE OF "MINESHAFT" BILL PELTON

"That crook won't get away with it this time!" Minnie cried as she burst into the detective agency later that evening.

"What are you talking about?" Mickey asked.

"Sylvester Slick, of course!" Minnie explained. "This afternoon Clarabelle and I looked around her attic and found a diary written by her grandfather, 'Mineshaft' Bill Pelton, the famous gold prospector. His diary talks about a strongbox full of gold nuggets!"

Minnie held out the battered old journal. "Clarabelle loaned this to me. Here, take a look."

Mickey leafed through the diary. *"A few days ago a new man came to join my team of miners,"* Mickey read. *"His name is Stephen Slick, and I don't trust him one bit. He spies on my every move. I'm getting the idea that he might be waiting for the right moment to steal the gold nuggets I've just discovered. So I've hidden the treasure in a secret place and have drawn a map of where they are on the next page—"*

"Here's the map," Mickey noted. "But there's no more writing. What do you think could have happened?"

"Maybe 'Mineshaft' Bill ran off to get away from Slick!" Minnie exclaimed. "Clarabelle said that he died shortly after returning from his last mining expedition. I'll bet he never had the chance to go back for the gold!" Minnie frowned. "But how did Sylvester find out about all of this?"

"Maybe Stephen Slick kept a diary, too," Mickey suggested. "He might have told the

story of the treasure and mentioned Bill's diary. Sylvester probably figured he could snatch the treasure if he ever found Bill's journal. Minnie, we have to warn Clarabelle!"

"Hey, take it easy," Minnie said. "I've already convinced her that Sylvester's just after the gold. Boy, was she furious! She called Slick right away to demand an explanation. He wasn't home, so she left a message on his answering machine. Naturally, he never called back. He didn't even show up for his date with Clarabelle this evening. That was the final proof that he was a fraud."

"Well, all's well that ends well," Mickey concluded. "Now we can get back to all our other investigations."

The detectives had just arrived at work that next morning when the door of the agency was thrown open. Clarabelle stormed through the doorway in tears.

"What happened?" Mickey asked, offering her a seat. He handed Clarabelle a handkerchief.

"A little while ago Sylvester came to my house to try to convince me to marry him," Clarabelle explained. "But I threw his flowers right in his face and told him to leave my house."

Minnie nodded. "Good for you!"

"But he just laughed and said, '*Your* house? Not for long! The mortgage on your home has been handed over to me!'" Clarabelle blew her nose loudly into the handkerchief. "Can

you believe it?" she cried. "Now I'm not in debt to the bank. I'm in debt to Sylvester!"

"But . . . how?" Mickey asked, astonished.

"A few days ago Sylvester asked me to sign our marriage license. He must have switched the papers when I wasn't looking!" she explained. "Instead of our marriage license, I signed contracts authorizing the bank to hand over the mortgage to him!"

"That cad!" Minnie folded her arms across her chest.

"He knows that I found my grandfather's diary and the treasure map," Clarabelle continued. "And he told me that if I don't give them both to him, he'll kick me out of my own house. And he has every right to do it! The only solution is to pay off my debt by the deadline. But I only have a few days left, and I'll never raise the money in time! Maybe the bank would have given me another month or so. But Sylvester never will. . . ." Clarabelle stopped and burst into tears.

"Hey, guys! Have you seen what a beautiful day it is outside?" said a happy voice behind them. They turned, and saw Goofy.

"It's so—" he went on, then stopped when he noticed everyone's serious faces. "Hey, what's going on?" Goofy asked.

Minnie sighed. "Do you remember when we were at Horace's party and I told you about Clarabelle's mortgage? Well, now she doesn't owe money to the bank. She owes it to Sylvester Slick!" she explained. "And if she doesn't repay her debt by the established date—that's three days from today—the cottage will belong to him. Slick says the only way he'll let Clarabelle stay in her house is if she gives him the map that leads to a treasure discovered years ago by her grandfather, 'Mineshaft' Bill Pelton."

"Uh, I don't really get the whole story," Goofy admitted, "but if there really is a treasure, why don't we go find it? Clarabelle could use it to pay off her debt."

Clarabelle, Minnie, and Mickey looked at each other. "You're right, Goofy!" Minnie agreed. "That's a great idea!"

"We don't have a minute to lose," Mickey put in. "We'll leave tonight to search for 'Mineshaft' Bill Pelton's treasure!"

"You can count on us, Clarabelle!" Goofy said.

"Actually, Goofy," Mickey said gently, "it might be better if you stayed here. We can't close the agency, and it would help us a lot if you looked after it while we're gone."

"Sure thing, Mickey," Goofy said happily. He would have preferred to join Mickey and Minnie on their adventure, but he knew how important it was to keep the agency open.

Once the others had left, Goofy leaned back in Mickey's chair. He put his feet up on the desk and folded his hands behind his head.

He looked out the open window, and spied Sylvester Slick walking down the street. "Hey, you swindler!" Goofy shouted angrily. He leaned far over the windowsill and shook his fist at Sylvester. "Don't even think you'll get Clarabelle's house so easily! Once Mickey and Minnie find the hidden treasure, Clarabelle will be able to pay off her mortgage, and you won't get anything!"

Chapter 4

A DANGEROUS ACCIDENT

Sylvester Slick had no time to lose. He knew Mickey and Minnie's reputation as private investigators. They never started anything they couldn't finish. If they decided to find the treasure, they'd get it for sure. Sylvester's only chance was to find it before they did, and to do that, he would need help.

Sylvester consulted his Palm Pilot. He had a list of all the biggest criminals in existence, but only one of them was capable of matching wits with investigators like Mickey and Minnie...Peg Leg Pete!

It'll probably take a big chunk of the

treasure to convince Pete to come along, Sylvester thought. Peg Leg Pete had been involved in almost every major crime that had happened in the city in the past ten years. If anyone could outwit Minnie and Mickey, he could. Sylvester took out his cell phone and dialed.

"If we find the gold nuggets, we'll divide them in half," Sylvester offered, once he had explained the situation to Peg Leg Pete.

Peg Leg Pete laughed so loudly that Sylvester had to hold the phone away from his ear. "Three quarters for me and one quarter for you!" he demanded.

Sylvester frowned. "You seem to have forgotten that if I hadn't called you, you wouldn't even know the treasure existed," he reasoned.

"Oh, please," Peg Leg Pete groaned. "If I hadn't given you advice on that fake telephone bill scam you were running, you'd be in prison right now, not hunting for treasure."

"All right, all right," Sylvester said with a sigh. "You win."

* * *

A few hours later, a car slowed to a stop across the street from Mickey and Minnie's detective agency. Slick and Peg Leg Pete planned to watch and wait . . . they were positive that the investigators would leave soon on their hunt for 'Mineshaft' Bill Pelton's treasure. Then Sylvester and Pete would follow them.

It was almost midnight when the door of

the agency finally cracked open. From the car, the two villains watched the detectives load their backpacks, some duffel bags, and a laptop computer into a Jeep. As the Jeep pulled away, Pete and Sylvester followed slowly, careful not to be seen.

Both cars sped up when they reached the highway.

The trip was long. Slick, who was driving, kept a close eye on Mickey and Minnie's Jeep. He had to keep his distance, though, or the detectives would realize they were being followed. Peg Leg Pete snoozed peacefully in the backseat. Every once in a while he would wake up with a snort, turn over, and fall asleep again. He needs his rest, Sylvester reasoned, so that he can figure out a plan for getting the gold nuggets.

But after driving several hours, Sylvester decided that Pete had rested long enough. "Did you see how much baggage they took with them?" Sylvester said loudly. "It looks like they're about to take a trip around the world!"

"Be quiet," Peg Leg Pete mumbled. "I can't hear myself think."

"Well, it's already dawn, anyhow," Sylvester answered. "That means it's your turn to drive. We decided that we would split the work, remember?"

"We are splitting it," Peg Leg Pete grumbled. "You're driving, and I'm thinking. I'm the brains of this operation."

"Look, I'm sleepy," Slick complained. "It could be dangerous if I fall asleep at the wheel."

"It could be dangerous if you keep talking," Pete replied.

Sylvester decided that he should drive and let Pete get his rest.

The two cars sped along a narrow and curvy mountain road. On the left there was a wall of rock and on the right, a deep ravine.

"Look at the beautiful sunrise," Mickey said, enjoying the scenery around him. He and Minnie were wide awake, as they had taken a long nap in the afternoon. Their Jeep was custom made for this kind of terrain, so the drive was very pleasant. Suddenly, Mickey's eye caught something in the rearview mirror.

"Hey, that car's been behind us for miles," Mickey said slowly. "Somebody's following us!"

"Let me take a look." Minnie pulled out her binoculars. She turned in her seat and focused on the driver in the car behind them. "It's Sylvester Slick," she cried. "And he's got a friend of ours with him in the backseat. Peg Leg Pete!"

"Oh, boy, that's the last thing we need! Slick must really mean business." Mickey gripped the steering wheel tightly. "Let's see if they can keep up with us!" Mickey stepped on the gas pedal.

Slick sped up too, but he was approaching a dangerous curve. As the Jeep zoomed away, Sylvester struggled to keep his skidding car from flipping over.

"Hey, what's going on?" Pete yelled as he was suddenly jolted awake.

"What's going on?" yelled the terrified Sylvester. "I'm trying to stop this car . . . b-b-before it heads into . . . the r-r-ravine!"

Slick slammed his foot on the brake. Even though the sun was shining in his eyes and

Pete was screaming in his ear, Slick managed to bring the car to a stop at the edge of the road.

Sylvester opened his door and found himself looking down into the deep ravine! He backed up and scrambled out on the passenger side.

Peg Leg Pete tried to squeeze out of the car through the sunroof, but the opening was far too small.

"Hey, get over here and help me out!" Pete screamed to his accomplice.

"Why, certainly," Slick replied. An evil grin spread over his face. "I'd be glad to help you, on the condition that you agree to split the treasure fifty-fifty."

Pete narrowed his eyes. "Don't even think about it," he growled. "I've got a foolproof scheme to get to the treasure before Mickey and Minnie. And if you don't help me, you won't get anything at all."

"What scheme?" Slick demanded. "I don't see how we can possibly get the gold now. Those two are obviously quite aware that we're following them."

"That's why you need my help more than ever," Pete pointed out. "What are you waiting for?"

Sylvester was hardly convinced that his partner had a brilliant plan. But without Pete, his chances of seizing the treasure were slim. With that in mind, he tugged as hard as he could to pull his great big accomplice through the car's sunroof.

Sylvester cocked an eyebrow. "Now, what's your plan?" he asked.

Peg Leg Pete dusted himself off. "I'll bet Mickey Mouse has put Goofy in charge of the detective agency while he's off looking for the treasure," he explained. "I'm sure he'll call his friend to see if everything is going smoothly and to tell Goofy where he'll be in case of an emergency. Tonight I'll call the agency pretending that I'm Commissioner Muttonchops," Pete went on, a sinister gleam in his eye. "I'll tell Goofy that I have to talk to Mickey about an important police matter and then ask for the address of Mickey's hotel. That knucklehead will definitely fall for it. And then all we have to do is snatch

'Mineshaft' Bill Pelton's map." He waggled his eyebrows. "What do you think? Brilliant, right?"

Sylvester shrugged. "Well, first we have to find a telephone."

"What do you think I am, an idiot?" Pete shouted. "I've got a cell phone!"

"Oh, of course, Pete." Sylvester rolled his eyes. "Where is it?"

"In the glove box of the car."

"That's what I figured," Sylvester said, tapping his foot impatiently. "So—why don't you go get it?"

But just at that very moment the car teetered, and began to roll downhill. Within seconds, it had tumbled to the bottom of the ravine.

"Uh," Peg Leg Pete said, "forget the cell phone. We'll just walk to the nearest town."

Chapter 5

A DEEP, DEEP SLEEP

"This mountain air is fantastic!" Mickey Mouse exclaimed as he and Minnie sat down to breakfast the next morning in the hotel restaurant. "I slept like a rock."

"Me too!" Minnie grinned. "And it looks like we lost Sylvester and Pete."

"I wouldn't be too sure about that, Minnie. I'd be worried even if Sylvester were by himself, but since he's joined forces with Peg Leg Pete, we should expect the worst. I'd like to leave the hotel soon, before they have a chance to catch up with us." Mickey reached for his orange juice.

"But how are they going to do that if they don't even have the map? Besides, even if they did come by these parts, they'd never find us. The Jeep is safe in the garage and we've asked the hotel manager to not give information about us for any reason."

"I still don't want to take any chances," Mickey declared. "One last piece of toast and then let's go!"

At the garage, before getting into the Jeep, Mickey checked once more to make sure everything was in its place: telephone, computer, compass . . .

"Oh, calm down," Minnie said with a sigh, "we double-checked everything before we left, remember? We have everything we need."

"I know. But it's better to be safe than sorry," Mickey reasoned. "We can't afford to lose precious time when we're traveling. Hey, where's the map, by the way?"

"Don't worry, it's right here in my jacket pocket—" Minnie gasped. "Oh no!" She looked at her partner. "Mickey, you know I

don't like practical jokes! Give me the map."

Mickey shook his head. "I don't have it," he said seriously. The detectives scoured the inside of the Jeep. Then they returned to the hotel room and searched the dresser drawers, the closets, and even the wastebaskets. But the map had disappeared.

Peg Leg Pete's plan had worked perfectly. Goofy fell right into his trap. When the crook had called, imitating Muttonchops's voice, Goofy revealed the name of the hotel where Mickey and Minnie were staying. Sylvester and Pete snuck into the detectives' rooms while they were asleep, found the map in Minnie's jacket, and stole it.

"It's all my fault. I was sure the map was safe," Minnie moaned. "Oh, poor Clarabelle! Now we have zero chance of finding the treasure."

"Well, things might not be that bad," Mickey corrected her with a smile. "Before we left, I scanned 'Mineshaft' Bill's map into the computer. I'll boot it up and show you the map on the screen."

"Mickey, you're really one in a million!" Minnie beamed at him.

Mickey smiled shyly. "Come on, Minnie. Let's get a move on," he said. "We've already lost a lot of time."

Moments later, the Jeep was on the road and they were speeding along, enjoying the beautiful drive.

"You know what this scenery reminds me of?" Minnie said. "A western movie! I wouldn't be surprised if we saw a cowboy riding up the road!"

"Wouldn't that be something!" Mickey answered. Just then he glanced behind him and frowned. "Well, I don't see a cowboy on horseback . . . but I do see two police officers on motorcycles."

"Two police officers?" Minnie twisted in her seat to look.

The officers flanked them with their powerful motorcycles. One of them motioned for Mickey to pull over.

Mickey pulled onto the shoulder.

"License, please," ordered the policeman who had pulled them over.

"It must just be a routine inspection," Mickey said in a low voice as he showed his license and registration to the officers.

"Everything seems to be in order," the police officer said, handing the papers back to the detective. "But you should follow us to the police station so we can check up on a few things."

"What for?" Mickey asked.

"This Jeep has been reported stolen," the

policeman explained, leveling his gaze at Mickey. "The owner, 'Mineshaft' Bill Pelton, reported the theft just this morning."

"But that's impossible," Mickey protested, struggling to keep calm. " 'Mineshaft' Bill Pelton was our friend's grandfather. And I'm sure that he never owned a Jeep, because he died many years ago. Hmm, some crook must have impersonated him using fake documents. And I'll bet anything it was Peg Leg Pete."

"Oh, *really*?" the policeman said sarcastically. "Now I've heard everything! Well, I guess we can clear this up at the police station."

"A quick phone call to Commissioner Muttonchops will clear everything up," Mickey assured the investigators once they had reached the town. Even though Mickey and Minnie's detective agency was well known in their city, nobody in this sleepy town hidden high in the mountains had ever heard of the investigators. "He'll confirm that we're telling the truth. Here's the number— it's 555-MUTT."

"I'm sorry," said the police sergeant after calling. "The commissioner is away from his office all day on an investigation. We can't reach him. In the meantime, I'll just have to keep you here." The sergeant locked the two detectives in a holding cell.

"Now what do we do?" Mickey put his head in his hands. "Sylvester Slick and Peg Leg Pete are way ahead of us. We might lose the treasure!"

But Minnie had an idea.

"Officer! Officer!" she called. The policeman walked to the cell. "Did you happen to see the man who called himself 'Mineshaft' Bill Pelton?" Minnie asked.

"Sure I did," replied the police officer. "I was here with the sergeant when Pelton came to report the theft."

"There's a way to prove what we're saying is true," Minnie explained. "All you have to do is look through your mug shots. That way you'll see that the person calling himself 'Mineshaft' Bill Pelton is really the crook I was telling you about."

The officer pulled out the mug shot album

and flipped through it. "My goodness!" he cried as his eyes fell on the photo of Peg Leg Pete. "That's him! That's the man who said he was Bill Pelton!"

The policeman apologized to the investigators as he unlocked their cell. He handed them the keys to their car.

"I thought they wouldn't let us out for ages!" Mickey Mouse exclaimed as he started up the Jeep's engine. "Good thing you had that clever idea. But now we have to make up for lost time. Those two should be about to find the treasure by now!"

"Well, just don't go over the speed limit," Minnie joked. "The last thing we need is another stop at a police station!"

Chapter 6

A DIFFICULT JOURNEY

As the sun rose in the sky, Minnie's heart began to sink. The road they were driving on passed through abandoned towns and dry fields. But luckily for the detectives, when they arrived at the last town on the map they saw a house with a tidy little garden. It looked as though someone still lived there.

Minnie knocked on the door. "Excuse me," she said to the old woman who answered. "Have you seen two strangers—one big and wide, the other tall and slim—pass by here recently?"

"Yes," the gray-haired lady replied, "and

they seemed to be in a hurry. They rushed
through town a few hours ago. If you want to
catch up with them, you'd better catch an airplane!"

"We could really use an airplane right
about now," Mickey said a few miles down
the road. "But I think we'll have to start
walking here!"

Mickey was right. The road suddenly came to an end, blocked by an enormous landslide. Even their Jeep couldn't drive over the huge mound of dirt.

"Let's hurry!" Minnie said courageously. "Look, no car could handle this, so they must be on foot, too. We still have a chance to get to the treasure before them."

The two detectives hoisted their packs onto their shoulders and began to trudge ahead under the burning sun. There was no trail to follow—they had to check the map again and again to keep from getting lost in the desert.

"Hey, Minnie, take a look at this," Mickey said. "It sure seems like they came by this way."

At their feet were the leftovers from a picnic. Greasy napkins, empty containers, and cans were scattered on the ground.

"Not only are they criminals," Minnie fumed, "they're litterbugs!"

"Maybe it wasn't them after all," Mickey noted. "Maybe the garbage was left by that fellow over there!"

In fact, not a hundred yards away, a man was walking slowly, his eyes glued to the ground. The investigators approached him. "Excuse me, sir," Minnie asked politely, "but did you happen to see two men go by this way?"

"Hey! Can't you see that I'm busy?" the man grumbled. "I'm looking for my mule. He got away yesterday. But I'll never find him if you go stomping all over his tracks."

The investigators looked at each other. What a strange man!

"Please, sir, it's very important!" Mickey said with a friendly smile. "We have lost two of our, um, friends. . . ."

"And how am I supposed to know where they are?" the man replied, obviously annoyed. "What do they look like anyhow, these friends of yours?"

"One is big and wide and the other is tall and skinny," Mickey said eagerly.

"Your description doesn't help me one bit," the man grumbled, scratching his chin.

The investigators didn't know what to think. Had they really taken a wrong turn?

Mickey turned to Minnie. "Maybe it's better if we backtrack," he suggested, "and figure out where we got mixed up."

"Oh, wait a minute," the old man said suddenly. "I *did* see those two you're looking for. If you help me find my mule, I'll loan him to you. With old Rufus you'll catch up with them in no time."

"It's a deal!" Mickey said. He shook the man's hand.

The three followed the mule's tracks in the sand, and before a half hour had passed, they discovered Rufus sleeping in the shade of a cliff.

After thanking the man, Mickey helped Minnie onto the mule, and the two were on their way again.

Chapter 7

THE TRAP

The trail leading to the X on the map was still very, very long. And the sun was very, very hot.

"Is it my imagination," Minnie asked, "or is this the slowest mule in the entire world?"

"And is it my imagination," Mickey added, "or did we pass that boulder once before?"

"It does look familiar," Minnie admitted.

Suddenly Rufus took off like a shot. He trotted straight through a break in the rocks. There they saw a water hole. The mule ran forward, impatient to plunge his nose into it.

While the mule drank, Mickey and Minnie filled up their canteens.

"Boy, I've never been so thirsty in my life." Minnie bent to the clear surface of the water and plunged her canteen into it.

The mule, which had just finished drinking, sat down on his hind legs. Then he lay down, stretched out by the water hole.

"Time to get up," Minnie said sweetly, giving the mule a gentle nudge.

The mule ignored her.

"Come along, Rufus," Mickey urged. "We need to get back to the trail!"

But the mule just let out an enormous yawn. Then he put his head on his forelegs and went to sleep.

"This is the laziest mule I've ever seen!" Minnie declared.

"Yes," Mickey said, nodding. "And I think our old friend knew that."

"What do you mean?" Minnie asked.

"Remember that I said I thought we'd passed by here before? Look." Mickey led Minnie back to the water hole's entrance. "There are two sets of mule tracks here. And they're identical. Two sets of tracks from one mule. We've been going around in circles!"

Minnie looked confused. "But why didn't we notice the water hole before?"

"Because you can't see the hole from the road," Mickey replied, leading Minnie to the spot where they had passed by before. Sure enough, high rocks on either side of the entrance blocked the view of the water hole. "You have to pass *through* the entrance to see the water hole," Mickey continued. "We never would have found it if our mule hadn't led us to it. I bet that Rufus knew the water was there all along. He just trotted over for a drink when he got thirsty."

"Are you saying that the old man knew that the mule would lead us away from the treasure?" Minnie sounded shocked.

Mickey nodded. "I'll bet Sylvester and Pete paid that old man to throw us off their tracks," he suggested.

"Oh, no!" Minnie cried. They took out the map and checked it.

"Well, at least we know we're not too far off the right path," Minnie noted, trying to be brave.

"Yes," Mickey agreed. "But we'll have to go the rest of the way on foot. It doesn't look like Rufus is going anywhere."

"I'm sure he can find his way home," Minnie said.

The detectives took to the trail in silence

in order to save their energy. After a short while, their foreheads were covered in sweat. Every once in a while they stopped to consult the map. Then they would begin again, slowly. Finally, they saw a high barrier of huge rocks far off.

Mickey looked at the map one more time and his eyes lit up.

"We're here! According to 'Mineshaft' Bill Pelton's map, the treasure should be right behind those rocks."

"But we still haven't caught up with Peg Leg Pete and Slick," Minnie pointed out. "Besides, I'm too exhausted to climb those rocks!"

"You won't have to," Mickey assured her. "The map shows a cave that cuts through the base of these rocks. It says we'll find the entryway between two boulders shaped like bears. Now let's see . . . where could those bears be?"

Minnie scanned the rock face with a sharp eye.

"There!" she shouted, pointing her finger. "Right in front of us!"

"By golly you're right! That rock looks just like a bear standing on its hind legs. And that one looks like a bear stretched on its belly!"

"Come on, let's go!" Minnie exclaimed.

Moments later, the investigators were at the base of the two big rocks. Minnie was right. They had found the spot indicated by "Mineshaft" Bill Pelton.

But there was one small problem. A huge boulder blocked the entrance to the tunnel, and now there was no way the two could get through.

"Are you sure this is the right place?" Mickey asked.

"Of course," his partner insisted. "I bet that those two villains must have rolled this rock down over the entrance after coming through here. We can't get in, but they can get back down the hill on the other side. Well, they don't need to worry about us now. We haven't the slightest chance of getting to the treasure!"

Chapter 8

DIGGING AND DIGGING

"When is this cursed sun going to set?" Sylvester Slick grumbled.

"Shut up and keep digging!" Peg Leg Pete ordered.

"Enough! I can't take it anymore!" Sylvester threw his shovel to the ground. "If you want this hole dug, then dig it yourself."

"Fat chance!" Peg Leg Pete snorted. "I'm standing guard," he pointed out. "We wouldn't want Mickey and Minnie to surprise us before we dig up the gold nuggets, now would we?"

"That seems pretty unlikely," Sylvester replied. "By now, that old man should have thrown them way off our trail. And besides, even if they haven't fallen into our trap, they'll never make it over the rocks!"

"I've known those two for a long time," Pete said, pointing his finger at Slick. "Too long. And I wouldn't be so quick to think we've shaken them."

Still muttering under his breath, Slick snatched up the shovel and began digging again.

"Why don't you check one more time to see if this is really the right place?" he suggested to Peg Leg Pete. "I have no intention of breaking my back just to find dirt, dirt, and more dirt!"

"If you'd stop blabbering, you wouldn't get so tired!" Pete said. "I'm sure that the treasure is right here. 'Mineshaft' Bill Pelton says so, right on the map: . . . *the treasure is buried at the foot of an oak tree ten feet high, with a heart pierced by an arrow carved on its trunk.* Do you see any other

ten-foot-high oaks around these parts?" Pete concluded.

Sylvester shrugged. "I'm so tired I can hardly see anything!"

"I'm going to say this one more time," Pete growled. "Dig! I'm getting tired of doing all this guarding for you."

From then on the silence was broken only by Slick's grumbling and the sound of the shovel driving into the dirt. Every now and then, Peg Leg Pete yelled for his accomplice to hurry up.

Suddenly Sylvester's voice echoed from way down inside the large, deep hole.

"Pete, come look at this! I think I found it!"

Peg Leg Pete approached, rubbing his hands greedily. Standing at the bottom of the hole, nearly ten feet down, Sylvester triumphantly brandished an old coin. "I must be near the treasure!"

"Idiot!" Pete shouted. "We're looking for gold nuggets, not coins!"

"Maybe Bill Pelton hid something besides gold nuggets!" Sylvester suggested.

"Let me look at that thing," Pete snarled,

leaning dangerously over the gaping pit.

"Be careful!" Sylvester warned him. "If you fall in, we'll never be able to get out of here. You ought to tie a rope around your—"

Too late!

Peg Leg Pete lost his balance. Desperately flailing his arms, he plummeted headlong to the bottom of the pit.

Pete sat up and brushed the dirt from his hair. "What are you looking at?" he growled at Sylvester. "Gimme that coin and keep digging," he ordered. He snatched the coin and scrambled to his feet. "Maybe you're right," he added, examining the coin. "This does seem like a really ancient—"

But looking at it more closely, Pete realized that Slick's discovery was not what it seemed.

"You blockhead!" Pete yelled. "A button, that's what this is! An old button. You better find 'Mineshaft' Bill's treasure, and fast, if you want your portion." He tossed the button on the ground.

"What are you trying to say?" Sylvester wailed. "We had an agreement!"

"Are you joking? I've been doing *all* the work around here!" Peg Leg Pete hollered. "And remember this: half of nothing is nothing. And that's exactly what we've found up to now, nothing! *You* just keep digging, Slick. *I* will climb out of here and keep watch."

But the crook could hardly lift his great mass off the ground.

"Help!" he cried after sliding down the pit's walls to the bottom several times. "Come and give me a push, you blockhead!" he said to Sylvester.

But Sylvester Slick wasn't much help. After all, he had driven for hours without a moment's rest. His arms were killing him from all the digging. But more than anything else, Peg Leg Pete was just too heavy.

"It's impossible!" Sylvester finally said after trying to help lift Pete up a couple of times. "I can't do it."

Peg Leg Pete folded his arms across his chest. "Then how are we getting out of here?" he demanded.

"I *did* tell you to tie a rope to a tree before

you tumbled down here!" Sylvester protested.

"Quiet," Pete said, holding his finger to his lips. "I hear voices. Someone's coming."

Peg Leg Pete would have known those voices anywhere. They belonged to Mickey and Minnie.

He turned to Sylvester, and whispered, "Well there's no need to worry. Mickey and Minnie would never leave without us—they're much too nice. I'll figure out a plan to convince them to pull us out. You can count on me!"

Slick was reluctant to trust Pete. But, as usual, he had no choice.

Chapter 9

AN AMAZING DISCOVERY

"If we didn't have to search for the treasure, it sure would be lovely to stop and admire the beautiful scenery!" Minnie exclaimed, looking around. "What lovely cliffs! Have you noticed how many different kinds of trees there are?"

"It must be that underground river we discovered that keeps everything so green around here," Mickey explained.

"I'm getting the feeling that luck is starting to turn our way." Minnie grinned. "If I hadn't slipped while we were climbing the rocks, we never would have discovered that cave, or that underground river inside that carried us all the way here!"

"I sure hope you're right," Mickey replied.

"Hmm, strange," Minnie noted, looking around her. "I don't see Peg Leg Pete or Sylvester anywhere. We really are lucky!" She peered at the map. "Let's see . . . an oak tree ten feet tall with a heart pierced by an arrow carved on its trunk. Hey, I see one over there!"

Mickey just grinned. "Do you really think that's the right tree?" he asked.

"Well, sure! I . . . oh, how silly of me! Of course not! In Bill Pelton's time that oak must have been no more than a little sapling. We'll have to look for a much older tree, won't we?"

Mickey nodded. "I think it's more likely to be . . . that one!" The detective pointed to an enormous oak tree. A heart with an arrow through it was carved into the trunk.

"Oh, Mickey, you're brilliant!" Minnie cried. "That's got to be the tree, I just know it!"

Mickey and Minnie got their shovels out of

their packs. And after digging for less than an hour, Mickey's blade hit something solid. It was the corner of the strongbox sticking out through the dirt!

"Hooray!" they hollered together.

"Help! Help!" they heard someone yell.

Surprised, Mickey and Minnie abandoned the strongbox for a moment to search for the voices.

"Watch out for that hole!" Mickey warned, pointing to the pit Sylvester had dug.

"So that's where they ended up!" Minnie cried, looking down into the hole at Pete and Sylvester Slick.

"Must be pretty cold down there, right, boys?" Mickey hollered to the two crooks. "I've got good news for you two. We've found 'Mineshaft' Bill Pelton's treasure. Looks like you two picked the wrong tree."

"Okay, okay, you win . . . this time!" Pete grumbled, shaking his fist at Mickey.

But Sylvester Slick just sat in the dirt, holding his head between his hands. His plan was ruined.

Seeing that the two scoundrels weren't

likely to escape the hole, Mickey and Minnie finished digging at a leisurely pace. There was only a little more work to do before they could pull the strongbox out of the ground. After so many years the box was a little tarnished, but it was still full to the brim with priceless gold nuggets.

"Let's call Clarabelle right away," Minnie suggested, reaching for her cell phone. "She'll be thrilled that we found the treasure."

"We shouldn't forget about those two down there," Mickey said, pointing to the hole.

"Do you think they'll be able to get out on their own?" Minnie asked him. "We can't just abandon them here."

"Don't worry, Minnie," Mickey assured her. "I'll just call a search and rescue squad that I happen to have the number for. It's called the police force."

Minnie smiled. "Now, that's a great idea!"

Chapter 10

THE MORTGAGE IS DUE!

Clarabelle had been humming to herself ever since she got the phone call from Mickey and Minnie. She was getting ready for the party she was hosting to celebrate the discovery of the treasure. She had already set out delicious little sandwiches, potato salad, and lemonade. As she was tasting the fruit salad, there was a knock at the door.

"They're here!" Clarabelle hurried to the door, wiping her hands on her apron.

But instead of her friends, she discovered . . . her ex-fiancé!

"Good afternoon, Clarabelle," Sylvester

said. "I see that you have prepared a little party. A good-bye meal? Or is it a welcome gift for the new owner of this house?"

Clarabelle scowled at him. "I think you better go home, Sylvester."

"Me? Go home? But I *am* home, my sweet." He smiled cruelly. "Surely you haven't forgotten that the mortgage is due today."

"I know it is!" Clarabelle shot back. "Today at noon. And it's five to noon right now!"

"Don't waste my time!" Slick hissed. "This house belongs to me now, so you had better gather your belongings and get out of here, otherwise I'll have to . . ."

Clarabelle ignored him and went inside the house. "Now let's see, where did I put that telephone . . . these cordless things! You never know where they'll end up next . . . Ah, here it is!" She handed the phone to Sylvester. "Go right ahead and call the bank," Clarabelle told him. "They'll tell you that the necessary amount needed to pay off the rest of the mortgage has already been deposited."

Sylvester Slick stared at her, his mouth open in shock. "What are you talking about?"

he demanded. "Last night Mickey and Minnie were still hundreds of miles away from here. Pete and I had to catch a plane to get here before them once we got out of that blasted hole. . . ."

Clarabelle laughed. "Don't you get it?" she asked. "Mickey and Minnie sold the gold nuggets and deposited the money in the nearest bank. Then they transferred the money directly into your account to pay off the mortgage. You're too late to get the house, Sylvester! Although you still have plenty of money in the bank."

Furious, the crook turned on his heels. At that very moment a sports car stopped in front of the house. Out popped Mickey, Minnie, Horace Horsecollar, and Goofy.

"Oh, you're not staying for lunch?" Horace asked Slick sarcastically. "What a shame! You'll be missing a beautiful party . . . and Clarabelle's house is such a nice place, too, isn't it?"

Sylvester just frowned and kept walking.

"We should call the cops!" Mickey said once Sylvester was out of earshot.

"No need," Minnie said. "Look!"

Everyone turned to see that two police officers had stopped Sylvester at the end of the block. They were escorting him to their police car.

"Well, at least he'll have some company in jail," Minnie observed. "Peg Leg Pete is there already."

"Come on, everyone," Horace said. "Let's

not stand around discussing criminals. Let's have a party!"

Everyone went into the house. And with all the good food, music, and dancing, the party was one nobody would soon forget. Especially Horace, because this time Clarabelle danced with him—and no one else.

"I ought to apologize," Clarabelle whispered into his ear while they danced. "I don't know what came over me and made me swoon over that crook."

"I could never be mad at you," Horace said to his friend. "When you think about it, it's really all because of Sylvester that you found your grandfather's treasure and paid off the mortgage."

"But the thanks really go to Mickey and Minnie! I have no idea what I should do to thank them . . . any suggestions?"

"Well, you've got so much money left over from your grandfather's treasure, you could get them practically anything," Horace pointed out. He thought for a moment. "Why don't you get them that spy-van they have been dreaming about for so long? The one with amplified microphones, motion detectors, bugging devices, surveillance equipment, and . . ."

"Horace, you're a genius!" Clarabelle interrupted him. "But don't say anything about it. I want this to be a surprise!"

"What are you two whispering about?" Minnie asked, approaching them.

"Oh, nothing too important . . ." Horace grinned at Clarabelle. "We were just talking about what great detectives you and Mickey are."

"Aw, gee, don't exaggerate," Mickey protested. But he looked rather proud.

"We may be good detectives," Minnie said, "but I still have two unanswered questions. First, how in the world did those two discover we had set out to find the gold nuggets in the first place?"

Goofy turned red as a beet.

"Uh, that was me," he admitted sheepishly. "I spotted Sylvester and I was so angry that I said a little too much. . . ."

"Okay." Minnie nodded. "So here's my

other question—how did they know where to find us, and the map?"

It didn't seem possible, but Goofy turned even redder.

"Aw, gawrsh," Goofy said, "that was me, too! One of those crooks called pretending to be Commissioner Muttonchops and asked where you were staying. I figured out what had happened when the real Commissioner Muttonchops called the next day. I'm awfully sorry," Goofy finished.

"Well, Goofy, those were honest mistakes," Minnie assured him. "What's important is that everything turned out fine. And if you hadn't been there to watch over the agency, we never would have been able to find Clarabelle's treasure in time. So thanks for your help!"

"Thanks to *all* of you," Clarabelle said warmly. "You're the best friends ever!"

FROM Mickey Mysteries

MYSTERY OF THE GARBAGE GANG

Chapter 1

MICKEY THE JOURNALIST

"Minnie," Mickey Mouse asked as he gazed at his partner's feet, "is it trendy to wear a pink shoe on one foot and an orange one on the other?"

Minnie looked at her shoes and sighed. "I'm afraid not," she admitted. "This is just like what I was telling you yesterday. I'm getting absentminded—I've been working too hard." It had been a rough morning for Minnie already. First, she watered the plants at the Mickey and Minnie Detective Agency with window cleaner. Then, she forgot to save her computer files and accidentally deleted two days' worth of work. "I can't keep up this pace much longer," she continued. "Ever since Inspector Sharp retired, it seems like all the lowlifes in the world have moved to town."

"What are you complaining about?" Mickey replied. "Business is booming! Besides, we *always* have a lot of work. After all, we're the best detectives in the city . . . maybe in the whole country."

"Yes, but—" A shrill ring cut Minnie off. "There's the phone again," she said with a groan. "It's been ringing off the hook. Let's stop answering it."

Mickey just laughed and picked up the phone.

"Hello?" he said. "Oh, good morning, Mr. Noble!" Mickey smiled, but his expression soon grew concerned. "What? What happened? You sound terrified. . . . Oh, I see, you've been receiving threats? Do you prefer to talk about it in person? . . . We can meet you at the newspaper offices in an hour. . . . Okay, see you soon!"

Mickey put the phone back in its cradle and began pacing the room, deep in thought.

"Who is Mr. Noble?" Minnie asked.

"He's the editor-in-chief of the newspaper, *The Herald*. He has a case for us."

"Great, that's all we need." Minnie rolled her eyes. "We already have more cases than we can handle. . . ."

"I know, I know. But how can we turn this one down?" Mickey shrugged. "Mr. Noble has always been a fearless crime fighter. He exposes injustices and criminals all over the city. . . ."

Minnie sighed. "You're right," she admitted. "Okay, here's an idea. You'll go to the appointment with Mr. Noble. In the meantime, I'll try to finish up our most urgent cases. I'll meet you as soon as I'm done . . . and I've changed my shoes."

"Sounds great," Mickey replied as he headed for the door. "If things are as bad as Mr. Noble made them sound, I'll really need your help."

When Mickey arrived at *The Herald*, he was shown immediately to Mr. Noble's office. Mickey could read the fear and exhaustion on the editor's face.

"My dear Mickey," Mr. Noble explained, "*The Herald* is a paper that isn't afraid to expose injustice; we write the truth and nothing but the truth. Last year we exposed a restaurant for serving food that had gone bad. The owner had to pay a fine and clean up his act. A few months ago, we published a story on a dealer who sold cars that polluted the air. As a result, the dealership was closed. We've fought countless battles like these. And we always win!"

"And naturally," Detective Mickey said, "these kinds of stories don't exactly make you a lot a friends, right?"

"Right. A few of the people we've exposed truly hate us, and they often seek revenge," Mr. Noble said seriously. "We receive a lot of anonymous letters and telephone calls."

"Unfortunately, that's one of the hazards of the job." Mickey shook his head.

"That's true," Mr. Noble admitted. "But no one has ever gone this far before."

Mickey frowned. "What do you mean, 'this far'?" he asked.

With a trembling hand, Mr. Noble pointed to a broken window.

"Someone tossed a rock through the window. There was a note attached." The editor opened a desk drawer and pulled out a piece of paper. "Whoever did this wants me to understand that this time the threats are serious. Here, read this."

He passed the note to the detective.

> *This is a warning.*
> *If you publish one more word*
> *against us, you can say good-bye*
> *to your beloved newspaper.*

Mickey couldn't hide his concern.

"Until today, none of the threats have ever been carried out," Mr. Noble explained, obviously disturbed. "But if they're bold enough to do this in broad daylight, who knows what they'll try next. . . ."

"We have to find whoever wrote this letter as soon as possible," Detective Mickey concluded. "We won't give him the chance to carry out any threats. Be brave, Mr. Noble. Starting now, the Mickey and Minnie Detective Agency is on the case."

Mr. Noble smiled. "You seem very sure of yourself," he said. "I like that. You have my permission to do whatever you think is necessary to take care of this situation. How do you plan to proceed?" he asked, leaning forward in his chair.

"Well, to start, my partner and I will pass ourselves off as your newest reporters. It will be much easier to observe any suspicious activity if we are working as journalists at *The Herald*."

"Great!" the editor exclaimed. "In fact, some of my reporters have left because they're worried about the threats. I can hire you to take their place and no one will suspect a thing."

Mickey knew that he could count on Minnie, but he thought this case might be too big for the two of them to handle on their own. He decided they would need help. Luckily, their good friends Horace Horsecollar and Goofy were available, and very eager to work for the newspaper. Goofy would work as a photo-journalist, and Horace as a typist. Mickey also recruited Donald Duck to sell papers and write opinion pieces.

Overnight, it seemed that *The Herald*'s new staff had made the paper better than ever. Detective Mickey was full of ideas for new columns. Clarabelle volunteered to cover the movie and theater sections, and Grandma Duck was going to share her best recipes. Mr. Noble was very pleased with all of the changes. He was certain that the newspaper's circulation would double in no time.

To be perfectly honest, there *was* the occasional disaster. Horace was a very *fast* typist, but not a very *accurate* typist. For example, Clarabelle's column, "Season's Best Films" became "Season's West Flims," while Grandma

Duck's "Deviled Eggs" became "Reviled Legs." And Goofy's photos were almost always out of focus.

But these little details didn't seem so important. Donald had arranged for radio ads to publicize the latest edition of *The Herald*, and sales of the paper were on the rise. In fact, some readers bought *The Herald* just for the fun of finding typographical errors and figuring out what was pictured in Goofy's snapshots. It seemed everybody was reading the paper and congratulating Mr. Noble on his latest success.